Dear Parent:
Your child's love of reading starts here!

Every child learns to read in a different way and at his or her own speed. Some go back and forth between reading levels and read favorite books again and again. Others read through each level in order. You can help your young reader improve and become more confident by encouraging his or her own interests and abilities. From books your child reads with you to the first books he or she reads alone, there are I Can Read Books for every stage of reading:

SHARED READING
Basic language, word repetition, and whimsical illustrations, ideal for sharing with your emergent reader

BEGINNING READING
Short sentences, familiar words, and simple concepts for children eager to read on their own

READING WITH HELP
Engaging stories, longer sentences, and language play for developing readers

READING ALONE
Complex plots, challenging vocabulary, and high-interest topics for the independent reader

ADVANCED READING
Short paragraphs, chapters, and exciting themes for the perfect bridge to chapter books

I Can Read Books have introduced children to the joy of reading since 1957. Featuring award-winning authors and illustrators and a fabulous cast of beloved characters, I Can Read Books set the standard for beginning readers.

A lifetime of discovery begins with the magical words "I Can Read!"

Visit www.icanread.com for information
on enriching your child's reading experience.

I Can Read!

READING
2
WITH HELP

THE LAST STAND

ROGUE FINDS A HOME

Adapted by Harry Lime
Illustrated by Boyd Kirkland
Based on the motion picture screenplay
written by Simon Kinberg & Zak Penn

HarperCollins*Publishers*

HarperCollins®, ☰®, and I Can Read Book® are trademarks of HarperCollins Publishers.

X-Men: The Last Stand: Rogue Finds a Home
Marvel, X-Men and all related character names and the distinctive likenesses thereof are trademarks of Marvel Characters, Inc.,
and are used with permission. Copyright © 2006 Marvel Characters, Inc. All rights reserved.
www.marvel.com
© 2006 Twentieth Century Fox Film Corporation
Printed in the United States of America.
No part of this book may be used or reproduced in any manner whatsoever without written permission
except in the case of brief quotations embodied in critical articles and reviews.
For information address HarperCollins Children's Books, a division of HarperCollins Publishers,
1350 Avenue of the Americas, New York, NY 10019.
www.icanread.com
Library of Congress catalog card number: 2006920159
ISBN-10: 0-06-082205-8—ISBN-13: 978-0-06-082205-7

1 2 3 4 5 6 7 8 9 10
❖
First Edition

The life of a mutant is not easy.

Humans fear you.

Your family does not understand you.

You have incredible powers,

but sometimes they are hard to control.

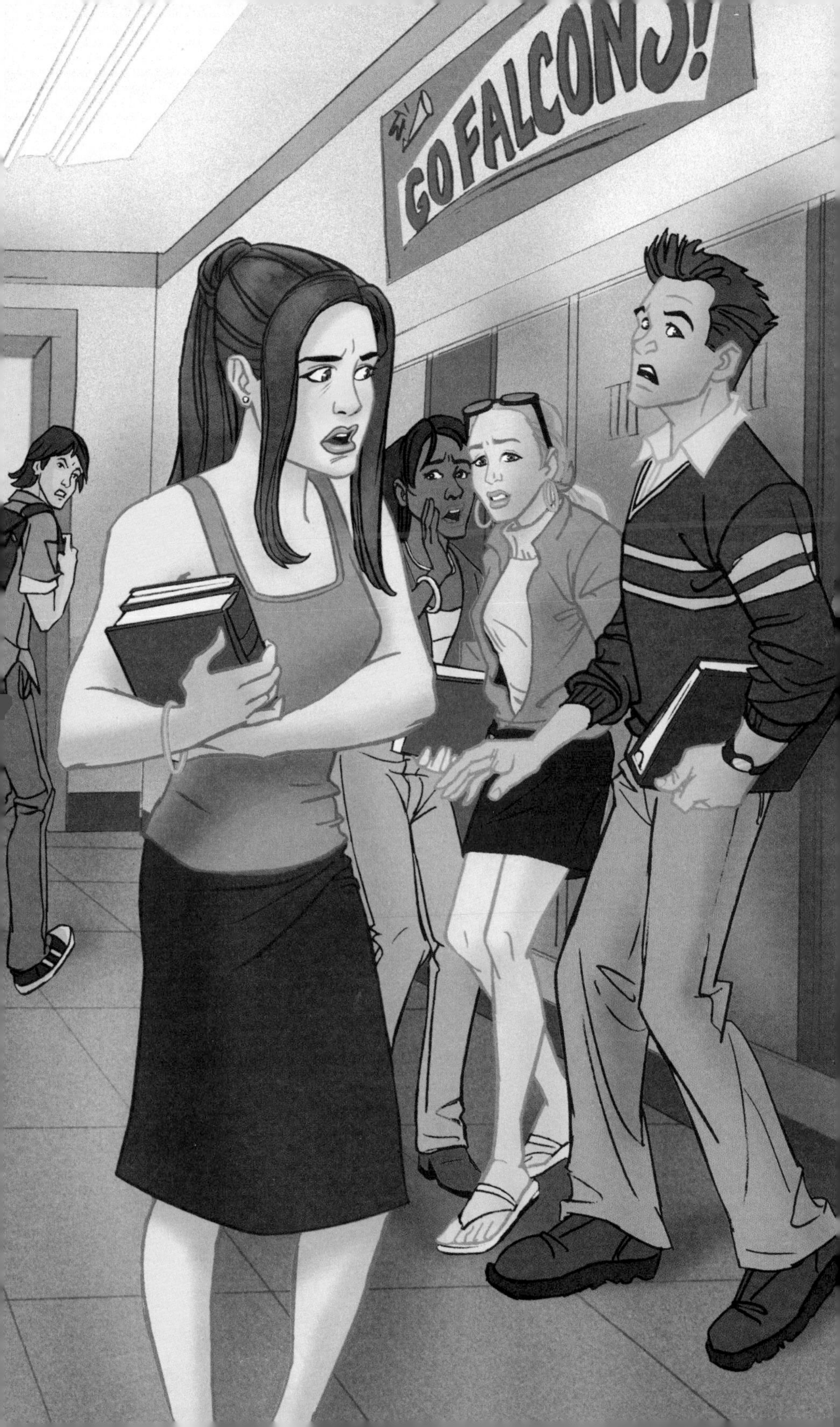
GO FALCONS!

Meet Rogue.

She can absorb the memories and powers
of anyone she touches.

But her touch is dangerous—
it can make people very sick.

Rogue did not always know
she was a mutant.
One day she was spending time
with her friend after school.
She touched him and almost killed him.
Rogue was so upset she decided
to run away.

Rogue had traveled for a short time
when she came upon something unusual:
a cage fight.

A man named Wolverine fought others
inside a cage for money.

When Wolverine began to fight,

Rogue was amazed.

She had never seen anyone so strong.

After the fight, someone tried to take

Wolverine's prize money.

Claws shot out of his hand as he pinned
the man against a post.

Rogue realized she had met someone else
with special powers.

Wolverine was a mutant, just like her!

From that moment on,

Rogue's whole life changed.

Wolverine agreed to travel together.

On their journey, they met other mutants.

When Rogue and Wolverine were attacked,

Storm and Cyclops came to their rescue.

The heroes took Rogue and Wolverine to the special School for Gifted Youngsters. *Everyone* there had a special power, and everyone there was a mutant.

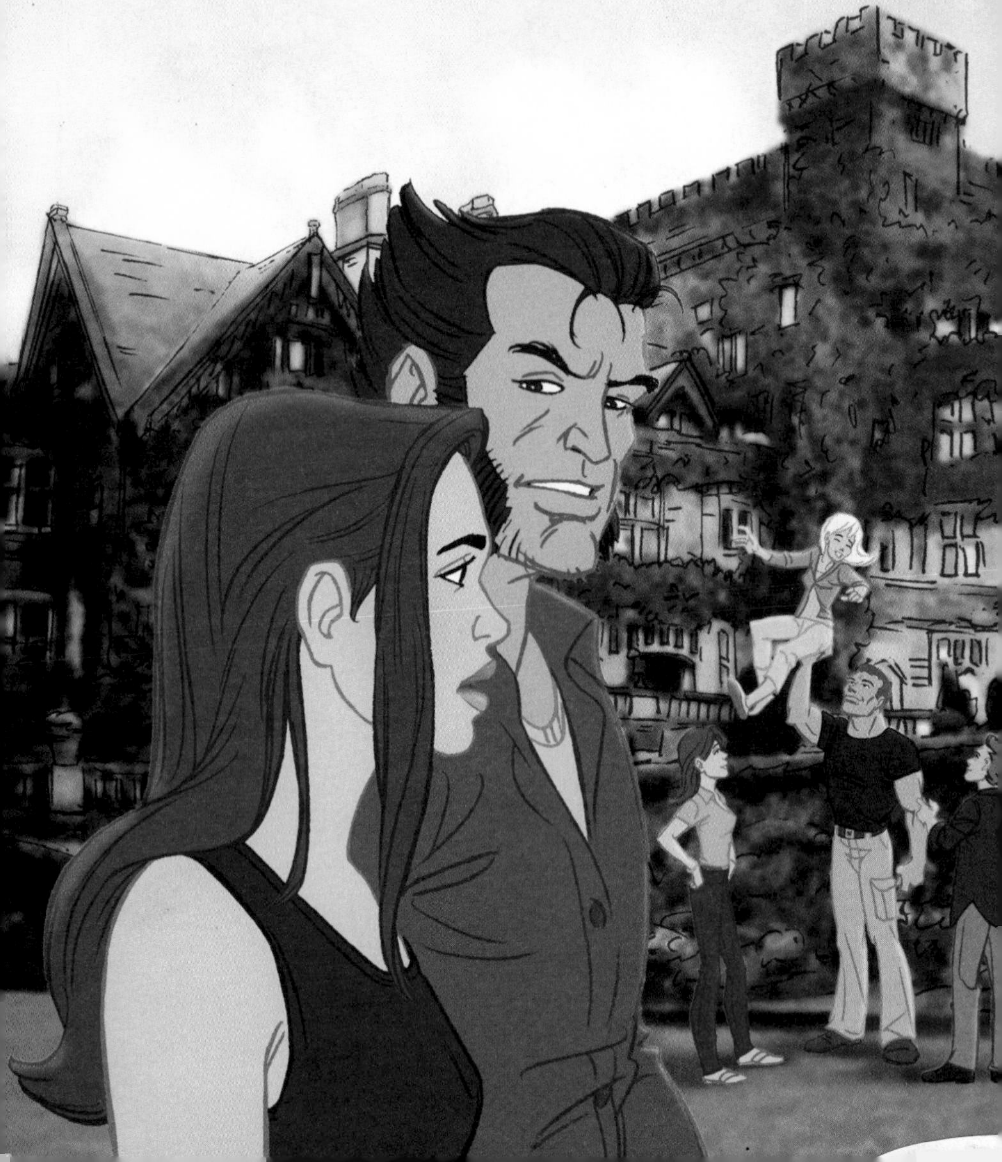

Rogue had finally found a place
where she felt at home.
For the first time, she felt comfortable
with her abilities.

One night Rogue heard
Wolverine having a nightmare.
He was screaming in his sleep.

But when Rogue tried to wake him,

she sucked the life right out of his body.

She could not do anything right!

Even though Wolverine survived, all the

other students knew what had happened.

They were all afraid of her.

Rogue was alone again.

Everyone avoided her, except Bobby.

Bobby was Rogue's closest friend.

Some people called him Iceman.

Bobby liked her,

even if she had dangerous powers.

He comforted Rogue when a difficult

mission turned her hair white.

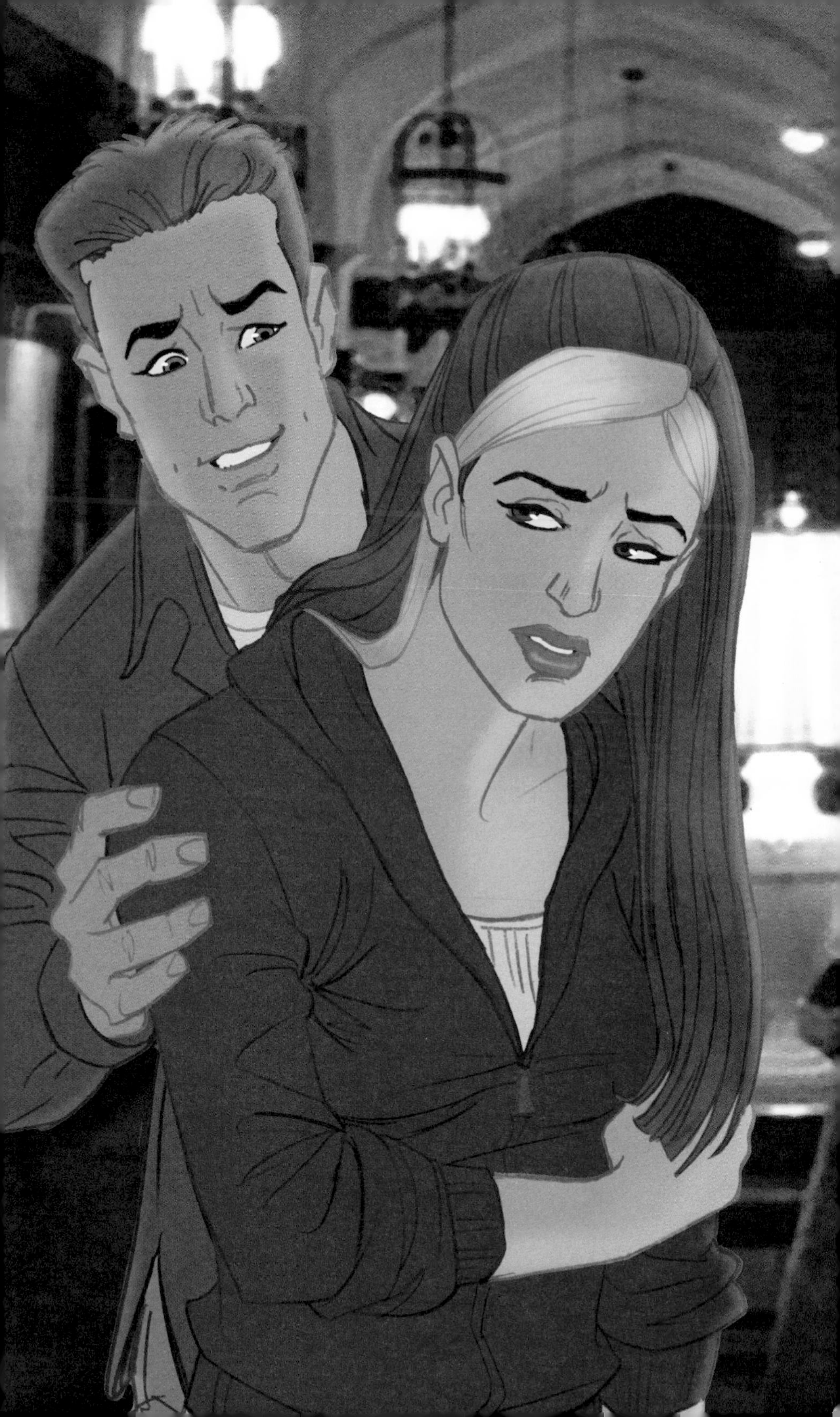

Still, Rogue wondered what
it would be like to be human—
to play with her friends like a normal girl.
Humans did not have to worry about
hurting people with their special powers.

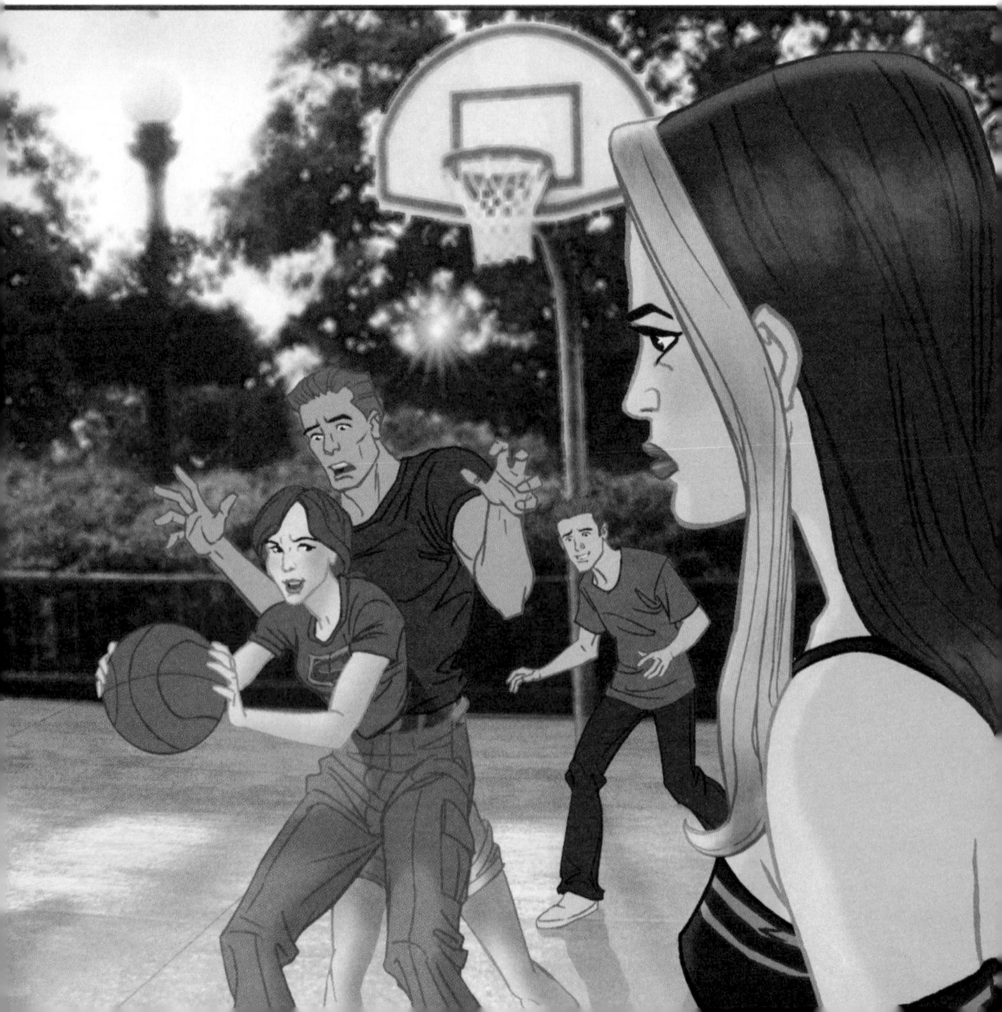

At school one day, Rogue could hear
Wolverine and Storm talking loudly.
They were talking to Beast
about a cure for mutants.
Rogue listened.

As the days passed, the teachers
at the school argued about the cure.
Storm thought it was a bad idea.
"There is nothing to cure!
What kind of coward would take it
just to fit in?" Storm asked.

But Beast understood why some mutants might want it—the life of a mutant was difficult.

"Not all of us have such an easy time fitting in, my dear," Beast said. "*You* do not shed on the furniture."

The week wore on and Rogue watched the news from the mansion's TV room. "Is it true? They can cure us?" she asked

Storm answered her quickly.

"No, there is nothing to cure.

There is nothing wrong with you!"

But Rogue could think of nothing else.

Finally! She had a choice.

If she took the cure,

she would never have to worry again.

She could live like a normal kid.

But how could Rogue leave the school?

All her friends were there.

If she left, she would miss the X-Men

too much.

When Bobby began to make
new friends, Rogue was sad.
If she stayed this way,
she would never be close to anyone.

29

Soon the X-Men prepared to leave.

They had to stop Magneto

and his Brotherhood.

And they needed Rogue's help.

She had an important decision to make.

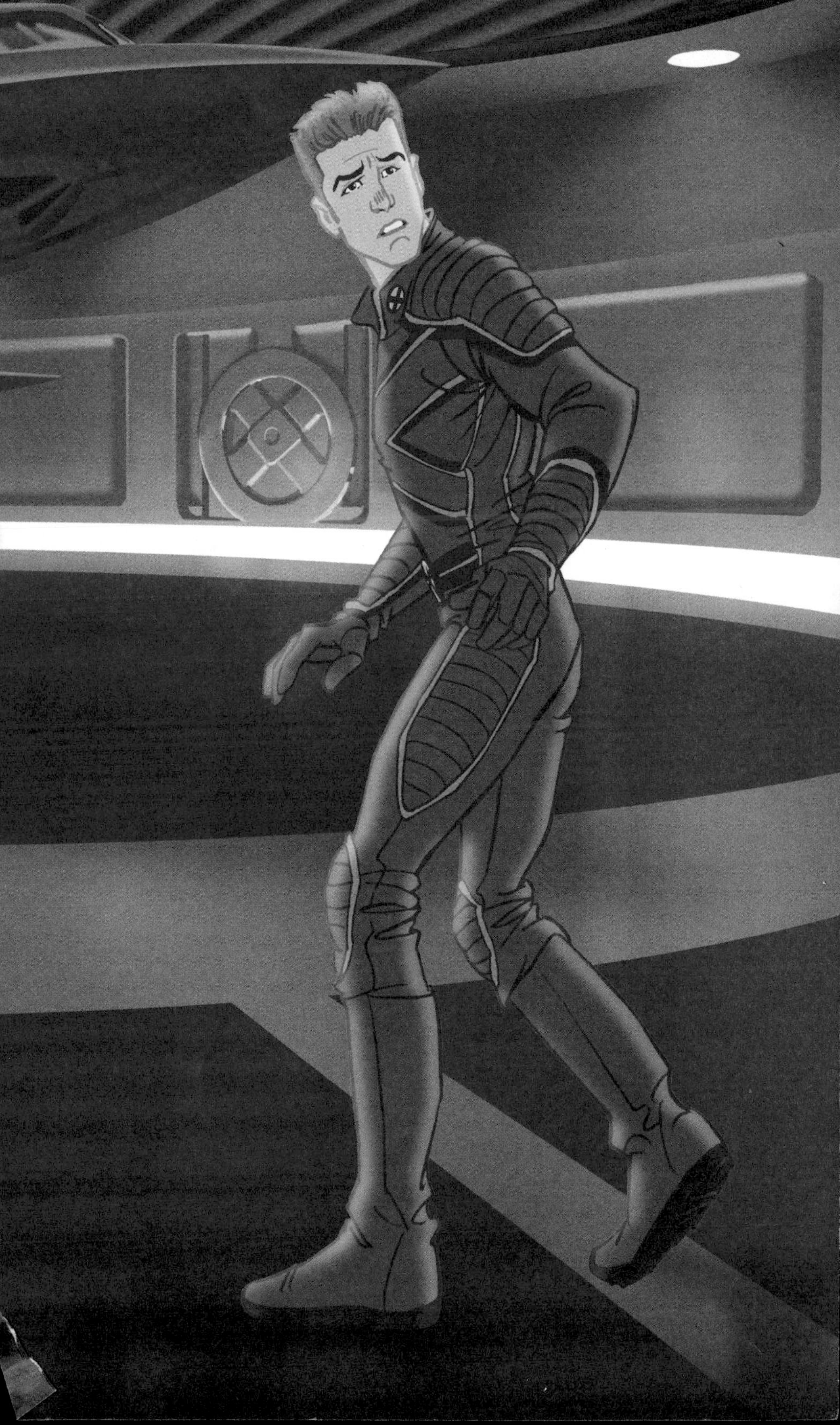

Bobby went to find Rogue in her room.

The X-Men were leaving for their mission

It was time to make a choice.

And for the first time in her life,

Rogue did.